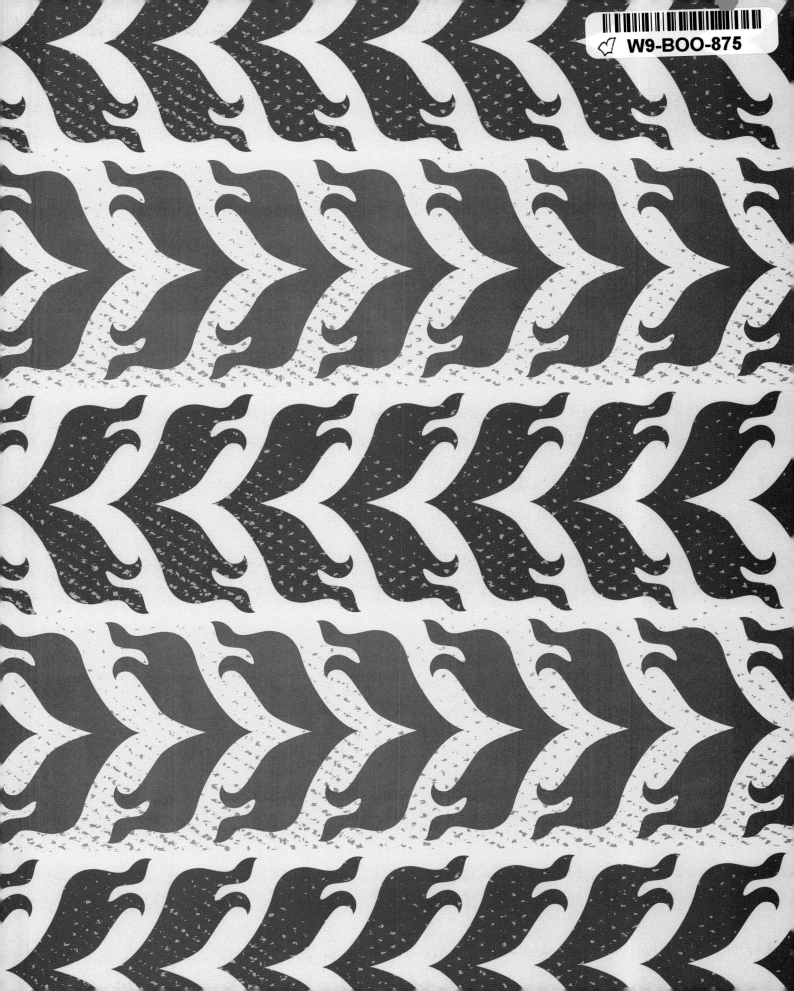

THE BIG BOOK OF BLAZE AND THE MONSTER MACHINES

A GOLDEN BOOK • NEW YORK

Welcome to Axle City, home of the Monster Machines!
Blaze, AJ, and their friends are always ready for a race—
and an adventure!

BLAZE

"Give me some speed!"

ACCELERATE
YOU ACCELERATE WHEN YOU'RE GOING ONE SPEED AND THEN YOU START GOING FASTER.

BLAZE

Blaze is Axle City's greatest hero and fastest racer! No one can **accelerate** faster than Blaze!

Blaze even thinks fast. He can turn himself into any machine—from a wrecking crane to a hydrofoil!

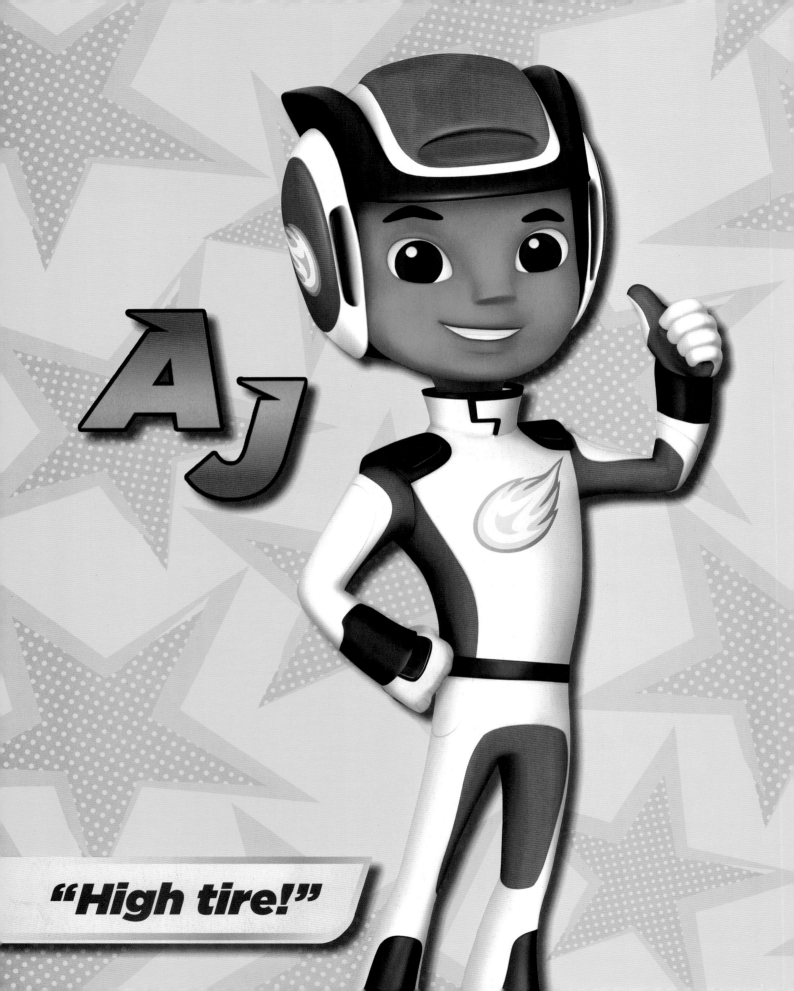

AJ

"High tire!"

AJ

This is Blaze's best pal and driver, AJ. AJ loves to drive fast, fly high, and speed into adventure! He can solve any problem using high-tech tools like skywriting gloves and a helmet visor.

CRUSHER

Crusher is a big truck but an even bigger baby. He'll do anything to win a race. Besides using his size and **mass** to bump other racers out of his way, he can build all sorts of things to help him cheat, like chomping robot sharks and messy banana launchers.

"Let's Pickle!"

PICKLE

PICKLE

Pickle is a little truck with a big heart. He's always trying to convince Crusher to do the right thing, but Crusher never listens!

STARLA

"Hoppin' hubcaps!"

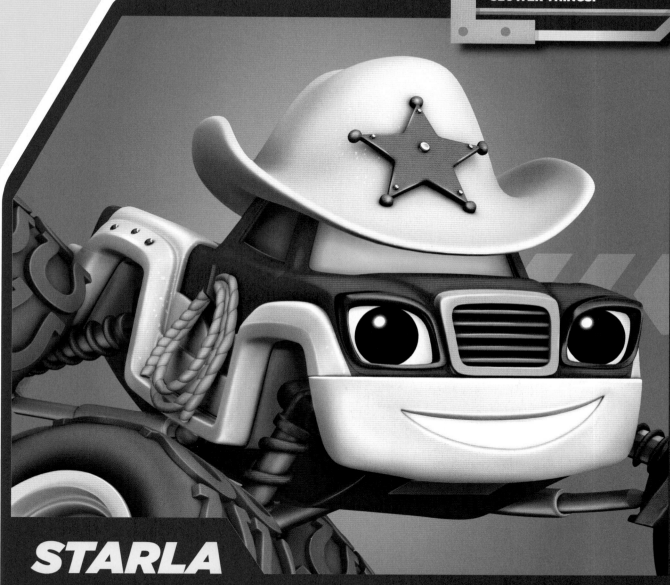

STARLA

With her lasso and sparkly hat, Starla is a hootin', hollerin' Monster Machine! She lives on a ranch with her piggy trucks. Starla can give herself extra **momentum** in a race by using her lasso to pull ahead of other racers.

STRIPES

"Tiger claws!"

STRIPES

Stripes is a tiger truck who lives in the jungle. He loves jumping, pouncing, and growling. Claws on his tires help him climb trees and grip the road.

DARINGTON

★ ★ ★

"Ta-da!"

TRAJECTORY
IS THE PATH
TRAVELED BY
SOMETHING IN
MOTION.

DARINGTON

Stunt truck Darington loves to do amazing tricks. He has a truly awesome **trajectory** when he zooms up ramps and flies through the air. But he doesn't always make a perfect landing.

FORCE
IS THE POWER USED TO PUSH OR PULL SOMETHING.

ZEG

Nothing makes Zeg the dinosaur truck happier than using **force** to smash and bash things. Zeg is big and tough, but he's a great friend, too!

GABBY

Gabby runs the Axle City Garage. With her trusty tools at her side, Gabby is the go-to girl for a Monster Machine tune-up!

MONSTER DOME

The Monster Machines zoom to the Monster Dome for races, chases, and high-speed action.

On your marks!
Get set!
GOOOO!

Blaze and his Monster Machine friends are rolling out on another awesome adventure. Ready?
LET'S *BLAAAZE*!

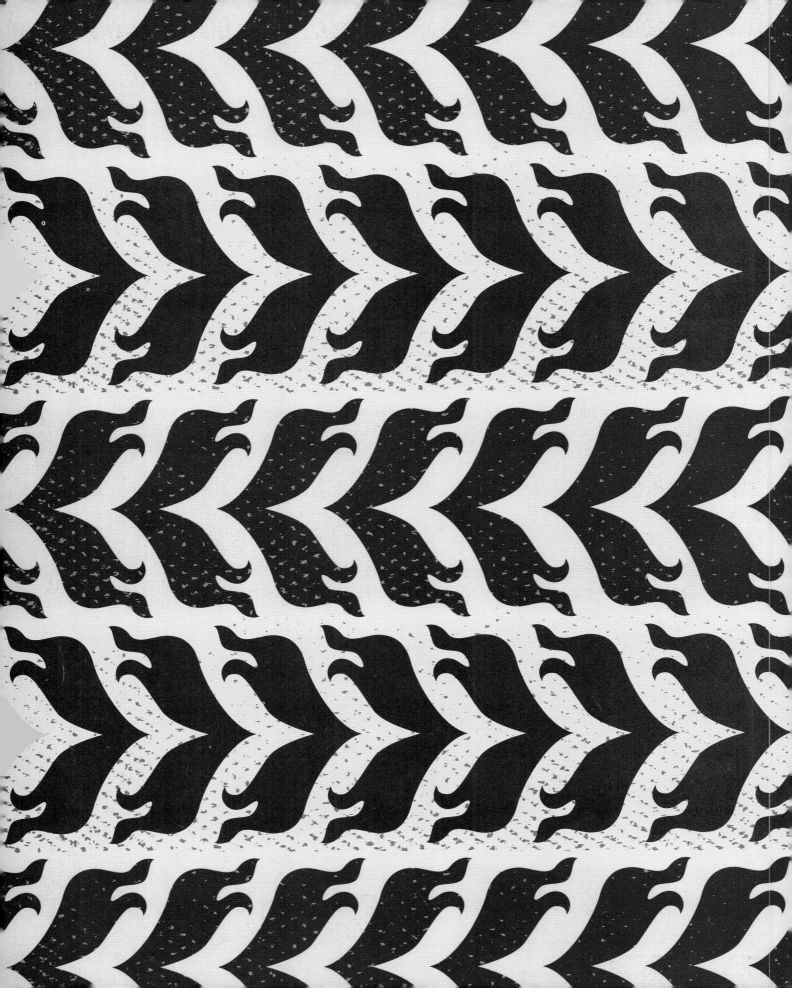